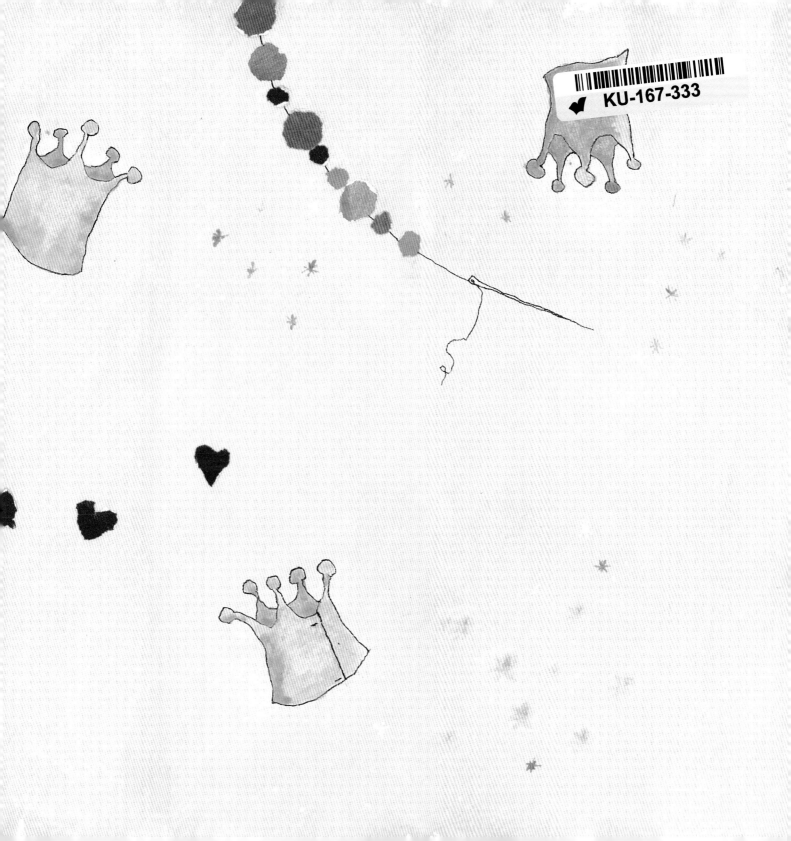

For all the princesses in the world

BLOOMSBURY
CHILDREN'S
BOOKS

First published in Holland in 1999 by Van Goor/De Boekerij bv, Amsterdam
with the original title 'En dan was ik de prinses'
First UK edition published in Great Britain in 2001
by Bloomsbury Publishing Plc
38 Soho Square, London, W1D 3HB

Copyright © 1999 Van Goor/De Boekerij bv, Amsterdam
Text design for UK edition: Sissel Sandve
English translation copyright © 2001 Sally Miedema

A CIP catalogue record of this book is available from the British Library
ISBN 0 7475 51103

Printed in Singapore

1 3 5 7 9 10 8 6 4 2

The Princess Gift Book

Tiny Fisscher and Barbara de Wolf

BLOOMSBURY
CHILDREN'S
BOOKS

I'm a princess. But I still look like an ordinary little girl.

Now do I look a bit like a princess?

My name is
Hoppity-hup

Stick your photo here

You can make a princess's veil from a piece of pretty material.

Make your own princess's purse.

You can make wonderful princess's harem trousers out of a big old skirt.

Princess's mules – you can make them with scouring pads.

Now I'm a real princess, look!

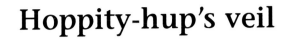

Hoppity-hup's veil

What you need:
★ a wide hairband
★ a long thin old scarf
★ a long imitation pearl necklace,
Christmas tinsel or ribbon
★ scissors ★ Sellotape
★ a length of 20 cm ribbon

Use Sellotape to stick the short side of the scarf to the underside of the hairband. Wrap the scarf once around the hairband. Now the scarf will fall over your hair and down your back. Cut a 15cm slit lengthways in the hanging end of the scarf. You can then drape the two halves over your shoulders.

Find the middle of the necklace and tie it with the ribbon to the centre front of the hairband. Put the hairband and the scarf on your head and hook the ends of the necklace behind your ears. You will look as though you're wearing very elegant long earrings.

Hoppity-hup's mules

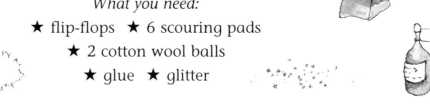

What you need:
★ flip-flops ★ 6 scouring pads
★ 2 cotton wool balls
★ glue ★ glitter

To make a high heel, stick 3 scouring pads together, with the rough side up each time. Make a second heel in the same way. When the glue is dry, stick one stack of the scourers to the underside of each flip-flop to make a heel. Sprinkle glitter onto 2 cotton wool balls and stick one on each mule.

Hoppity-hup's top

What you need:
★ a bikini top ★ 12 pieces of ribbon
(of different lengths, from 5 to 15 cm long)

What you can also use:
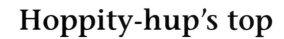 ★ a ballet costume or swimsuit ★ large beads

Put on the ballet costume or swimsuit (if it's hot weather, then don't bother). Tie the ribbons onto the bikini top and put it on. If you have some beads, you can thread a bead onto each ribbon. Make a knot at the end of the ribbon, otherwise the bead will fall off. If your bikini doesn't have a suitable place to tie the ribbons, then you can use strong Sellotape to stick the ribbons to the inside of the bikini top.

Hoppity-hup's harem trousers

What you need:
★ a grown-up's old skirt
★ 2 ribbons or strips of material
★ a belt

Put on the skirt and fasten it at the waist with the belt.
Fasten the skirt at both knees with a ribbon.
This will make the skirt puff out at the knees, making
a perfect pair of oriental harem trousers.

Hoppity-hup's handbag

What you need:
★ a marble bag/shoe bag or else a
square of material about 20 by 20 cm
★ beads, buttons, dried beans or uncooked macaroni
★ a length of ribbon

Fill the bag with the beads, buttons, dried beans or uncooked macaroni,
then tie it up with the ribbon. Or put the beads, buttons, or other filling
onto the middle of the piece of material. You can make this into a bag
by gathering the corners together and tying the ribbon around them.

Extras

To complete your princess's outfit, you can cut out and stick a spot of red paper in the middle of your forehead. Or you could draw a small red spot with lipstick or greasepaint.

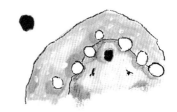

Oriental princess's customs

Oriental princesses sit or lie on a scattering of soft and colourful cushions.
Oriental princesses drink tea out of pretty teacups and eat Turkish delight or raisins.

HOPPITY-HUP

In a warm, dry sandy land, far, far away, stood a fabulous
sandcastle. Here lived the sultan with his wife and four daughters.
The sultan was short and fat with an enormous nose, thin spiky
hair and stumpy legs. He found this most unfair. After all, a sultan
was supposed to look strong and powerful. That's why he never left
the castle without a mountainous turban on his head and always
tottered around on high platform shoes. He also stuffed lots of
shoulder padding under his coat so he would look strong and tough.
And when he spoke, he tried to make his voice sound like thunder
and he hardly ever laughed. Sultans definitely
don't laugh, he decided. As well as all this he was horribly stingy.
On the first day of the month he would have the grains of sand in his
kingdom carefully counted just to make sure they were all still there.
'And you're not allowed to play with the sand!' he screamed
every time at his daughters. 'That's not what it's for!'

The sultan's wife was quite different. She was
tall and rather thin. She couldn't care less
about all that sand. She would giggle, and
chuckle, and burst out laughing - all at the
drop of a hat - much to the annoyance
of the sultan.
'Stop that childish sniggering!'
he would thunder.
But his wife would always giggle
for just a couple of seconds
longer, because she could
never stop straightaway.

Three of the sultan's daughters were the same age and looked exactly alike. As a matter of fact, they were triplets, and each had her own tower. They were called Millicent, Mildred and Minerva and they always went round together. As nobody could tell which was which, not even their own father and mother, they were just called Mi, Mi and Mi.

This was particularly convenient when they had to be sent for. Then you could hear 'Mimimi!' all over the castle.

When the three princesses were nearly grown up, a new little sister arrived quite unexpectedly. The sultan was most displeased. 'That means I'll have to order another tower to be built,' he grumbled.

The new little princess was called Hup, because when it was time for her to be born, her mother kept crying out impatiently, 'Hup, hup, giddy-up!' The sultan had feared it would be triplets all over again as that would have meant having three more towers built.

Little Hup was always full of fun and beans, which was quite unexpected with a father like the sultan. 'You keep getting in my way hopping around like that...you should be called Hoppity-hup instead,' complained the sultan one day.

'Hee-hee-hee,' his wife giggled. 'Hoppity-hup! Lovely!' From then on everybody called the little princess Hoppity-hup, except her father, of course. When Hoppity-hup was four years old she was allowed to go outside. In the golden carriage, way up high on top of Casper, the castle camel, the princess couldn't believe her eyes. 'What a lot of sand,' she cried.

'Yes, and it's all mine!' said the sultan, smiling proudly. 'I've got so much sand you can't even see where my country ends. My country goes on forever!'

Hoppity-hup was dumbfounded. Sand, sand and more sand — even the houses were made of sand.

But as they got further away from the castle, Hoppity-hup saw people who lived under rooves made of cloth.

'Don't those people have houses?' she asked in surprise.

'No,' her father answered, as if this was perfectly normal.

'Why not?'

'Because they have no money to buy sand.'

Hoppity-hup looked across the vast sand plain.

'Oh...'

The years passed by. Hoppity-hup grew up into a beautiful young girl with chestnut red hair and shining brown eyes.

Her sisters, in the meantime, no longer lived in the castle. They were married to John, Jodi and Jerome, spotty-faced prince triplets from another sandy country.

Yuk, thought Hoppity-hup, just imagine having to marry a prince like them. She'd never do that. She would have liked to visit her sisters, but her father wouldn't let her. After that one trip on Casper she had never been outside the castle walls.

'Why don't we ever go out?' Hoppity-hup kept grumbling.

'Because you're too curious!' her father would shout. 'That's dangerous!'

Hoppity-hup simply could not understand this.

One day she thought, if daddy won't allow me outside the castle, then I'll sneak out!

Very early next morning she crept past the snoring guards and out of the castle gate.

She looked around her wide-eyed. She saw men pushing carts, women with baskets on their head and donkeys with bags on their back. And she still saw people without a home.

How terrible! she thought rebelliously. How can Papa approve?

The next day Hoppity-hup found a flower behind her door, together with a little note.

'Will you come out to play?' it said. Nothing else.

Hoppity-hup went red with excitement. Nothing as exciting had ever happened to her. However did that little note get there?

She quickly hid it and went downstairs to breakfast.

'Hello Mum, hello Dad!' she cried merrily.

'Mmm,' her father mumbled grumpily.

'Good morning, darling!' her mother giggled. 'Boiled egg?'

The sultan's wife missed her other three daughters terribly
and each day she hoped for a letter.

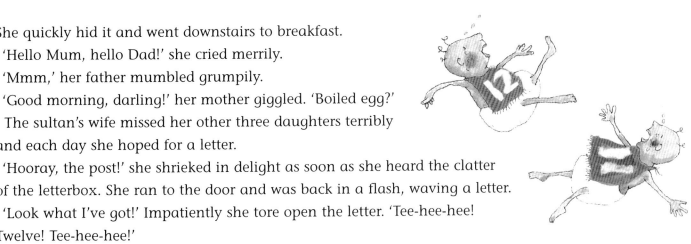

'Hooray, the post!' she shrieked in delight as soon as she heard the clatter
of the letterbox. She ran to the door and was back in a flash, waving a letter.

'Look what I've got!' Impatiently she tore open the letter. 'Tee-hee-hee!
Twelve! Tee-hee-hee!'

She dropped the letter, ran outside roaring with laughter, and rushed towards Casper the camel.

'What's going on now?' thundered the sultan.

Hoppity-hup picked up the letter. 'Mum,' she read out loud. 'We've just had twelve babies and
we can't keep them quiet. Come quickly. Mi, Mi and Mi.'

The sultan clasped his hands to his head. 'Twelve! Oh no! Then I'll have go on a trip, to buy
new sand for twelve new towers!' And he ran out without even saying goodbye.

'Dad,' Hoppity-hup called out after him. But her father didn't hear.

The princess sighed.

Dad gone. Mama gone, Casper gone. Then I'm going too, she thought. And she
just walked out of the castle gate, cool as can be. She walked through the village,
past all the houses and past the people without houses.

I wish I could build a castle for them, she thought.

She knelt down and buried her hands in the warm sand.

She made a little pile, but it just fell in.

She tried again. It fell in once more.

'Are you playing?' said a soft voice suddenly.

The little princess looked up in surprise and saw a boy with a laughing face and two merry dimples in his cheeks.

'No, I want to build a sandcastle, but it keeps falling in. Can you help me?'

'But surely your father won't allow that!' the boy said, shocked.

'How do you know who my father is?'

'I s-saw you w-wandering around yesterday m-morning,' the boy stammered.

'Did you write that letter?'

The boy nodded shyly. 'I crept inside the palace,' he whispered.

'That was brave of you!' Hoppity-hup took his hand. 'Come on, let's build a sandcastle. Anyhow, my father's not here.'

The boy hesitated.

'Please?' Hoppity-hup begged.

Reluctantly, the boy brought her to a well. Here he showed Hoppity-hup how to make firm walls out of sand and water for a sandcastle.

'Oh, how clever!' cried Hoppity-hup.

'You can do it too,' the boy said.

A little girl stood watching them, her eyes wide with astonishment. After a while she walked hesitantly over to Hoppity-hup and tapped her softly on the shoulder. Hoppity-hup turned round in surprise.

'May I live in that castle when it's ready?' the little girl whispered shyly.

'Of course!' said Hoppity-hup. 'Do you want to help us fin-?'

'What's going on here?' a voice thundered.

There was the sultan, with his guards and a whole herd of camels. Hoppity-hup shrank back.

'I … I thought you'd gone out!' she stuttered.

'Quite beside the point!' the sultan boomed.
'How dare you mess around with my sand! What's this
monstrous piece of work?'

He pointed at the sandcastle in disgust.

'I built that,' the boy said quickly.

'And I helped.' Hoppity-hup chipped in bravely.

'And I'm going to live in it,' whispered the little girl.
The sultan went quite pale. 'How dare you!'
He clenched his fists and stomped about in the sand.
'Guards, take them away!'

The sultan flapped his arms up and down wildly. So wildly
that his coat burst open and shoulder padding flew up into the air.

The guards started to giggle nervously.

'Do as I say!' the sultan shrieked.

The guards turned red in the face, bit their lips and wobbled backwards and forwards.

'Don't just stand there like a pack of idiots!' the sultan yelled in desperation. Furiously he stamped
his feet again in the sand. Just at that moment his platform shoes split in two, and to make matters
worse, his turban fell off his head!

Then the guards couldn't contain themselves any longer and burst out laughing.

'Well, dash darn and blow!' roared the sultan. He grabbed at his turban
and tried to keep his balance on his broken shoes. But it was too late.

Everyone had seen the sultan for what
he really was: a silly, petty little man.

'Ha, ha, and he calls himself
sultan!' cried one of the
guards. 'Why don't we just
call him Softie!' Everybody
doubled up with laughter.
Even the camels' knees
wobbled with laughter.

'Oh dash it and darn it all' the sultan wailed. He buried his head in the sand,
so he didn't have to hear all their laughter. Shrieking with mirth, the guards
left for the village, where the story spread like wildfire.

The princess, the little girl and the boy stood there in dismay.
The sultan suddenly looked so helpless, with his head in the sand.
  'Oh, poor thing...' the little girl whispered.
  Hoppity-hup went over to her father and helped him up. Clumsily,
the sultan wiped the sand off his face.
  'Dash it all,' he said, giving a little sob.
  'Mister sultan,' asked the little girl, pulling at his trouser leg, 'do you want to play with me?'
  'Do you know who I am....' the sultan started saying sulkily.
  'Cooee!' they heard suddenly.
  There was Casper jogging along towards them, one laughing granny, three chattering
Mi-mummies and twelve bawling babies all piled up on top of his back.
  Three weary-looking princes rode up behind.
  'My poor little sultan, what a sight you are,' his wife giggled.
'Now you can't go round looking like that, can you?'
Firmly she picked up his clothes from the sand and
helped him get dressed. 'There we are, all ready.'
  Shamefaced, the sultan just stood where he was.
'My shoes are broken,' he whined.
  'Dad,' sighed Hoppity-hup. 'Stop fussing.
Will you help us finish this castle?'
  'Ooh, can we help too?' the Mi-sisters chorused.
  The three princes looked gloomily at one another,
and said, 'Shall we just get on with some governing?'
  'No,' the sultan said to Hoppity-hup. 'Finish it yourself.'
But for the first time he let the children play with the
sand. Not wholeheartedly, because that was something
he still had to learn. And he couldn't resist secretly
making sure no one put any of it into their pocket!

The End

Make your own princess's hat with stiff paper.

Stick your photo here

You can make real princess's cuffs with plastic beakers or paper cups.

Make a pretty bodice with ribbons.

Decorate your skirt with ribbons.

You can also print designs on your skirt.

My name is Rosalie

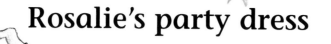

Rosalie's party dress

What you need:
★ a green T-shirt or jersey with long sleeves
★ white throwaway beakers
★ about 4 metres of thin white elastic or ribbon
★ a long pink skirt or sheet
★ a white belt or ribbon ★ tights ★ scissors

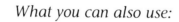

What you can also use:
★ stickers ★ 2 potatoes cut in half
★ a knife ★ paint ★ a cushion
★ a large piece of velvet

Put on your jersey and tights.

To make flared cuffs, ask an adult to help you cut the bottoms off two plastic beakers. You can decorate them with stickers. To put on your perfect princess cuffs, put a hand through the narrow end of each beaker.

Ask an adult to wind the elastic or ribbon a few times around the top part of your body. Starting from the top it should be crossed over several times before being fastened at the back. Make sure it isn't too tight.

To make a princess bustle under the back of your skirt, tie on a cushion before putting on the skirt or wrapping the sheet around yourself. Fasten them at the waist to keep them up.

If you're allowed to, you can decorate the skirt with little hearts and other shapes by making potato prints. Ask an adult to cut out your design on half a potato. Dip it into paint, then print it on your skirt. Let the paint dry before you put on the skirt. You can also loop a scarf or pieces of pretty cloth around the skirt. Attach them with safety pins. If you have fixed a cushion under the back of the skirt before putting it on (see picture on the page opposite), you will look even more like a fairy-tale princess.

As a finishing touch, make a cape by throwing a large piece of velvet around your shoulders. Fasten it at the front with a brooch, safety pin or clothes peg. If you need help, ask an adult.

Rosalie's hat

What you need:
★ a sheet of stiff pink paper
40 cm by 20 cm
★ 3 strips of material 20 cm by 10 cm
★ Sellotape ★ stapler ★ pencil
★ scissors ★ paint or stickers

Take the paper and roll it into a cone (see picture). Stick the edges together with Sellotape. Put the pointed hat on your head and mark where your ears touch the hat. Staple a strip of material to each side where you have marked them, so that you can fasten the hat under your chin. Decorate the hat with paint or with stickers. Stick the last strip of material to the top of the hat with Sellotape.

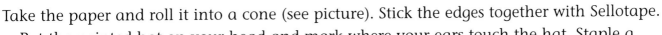

Rosalie's shoes

What you need:
★ ballet or gymshoes
★ 2 lengths of elastic 2 cm by 20 cm
★ stapler
★ 2 pieces of coloured or painted
cardboard 15 cm by 15 cm
★ Sellotape

To make elegant princess points for your shoes, bend over two corners of the cardboard (see picture). Insert your ballet or gymshoe into the point you have made. Now Sellotape the cardboard together so that it fits snugly round the shoe. Repeat for the other shoe.

Put on your shoes and push each one gently into a cardboard point. Staple one end of the elastic to a corner of the cardboard (see picture below). Take the other end round the back of your heel and staple it to the other corner. You may need to take the cardboard off your shoe to do this. The elastic should hold the cardboard point firmly over your shoe. Cut off any left-over elastic.

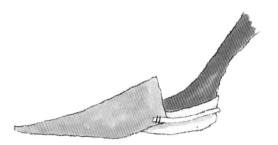

Princess Rosalie's customs and games

When princesses like Rosalie greet a king or queen, they curtsy by slightly bending their knees. At the same time they raise their skirt a little.

Princesses like Rosalie love dancing. Especially if they can whirl round in a circle holding hands with friends!

Rosalie

Once upon a time there was a princess who believed she was so ugly she didn't dare look in the mirror. This was rather odd, because really she was very pretty.

Her fair hair was like a halo of golden rays round her face. She had clear greeny-blue eyes and a funny little turned up nose.

Even her name was pretty - Rosalie.

So why did the princess think she was so ugly? Well, it's a long story…

When Rosalie was very small, her mother died. The king, who had loved his queen dearly, was nearly beside himself with grief.

For weeks on end he didn't sleep, he didn't eat and he didn't speak. All he did was weep.

The only time he felt a little less sad was when he looked at Rosalie, because she looked so like her mother.

The years passed by. One day Rosalie sighed and said, 'Dad, you're awfully sweet, but life is very empty without a mum around.'

The king gulped. But his daughter's happiness came first and straightaway he put an advertisement in the paper:

Wanted urgently: Mother for princess.
Only ladies with no children need apply.

The king got hundreds of letters. Most of them were dull and dreary.

But suddenly he saw a gold-coloured envelope. The king opened it up and immediately he was enchanted by the sweet-sounding words. He wrote back, 'You sound like the very thing. Come over as soon as you can, greetings from the king.'

The writer of the letter arrived that same afternoon, and was so beautiful the king nearly fell off his throne. Her delicate faced was framed in glossy, black hair and she had bewitching deep blue eyes. She had a sweet smile and made funny jokes.

'Will this mum do?' the king asked his daughter.

Rosalie didn't need telling twice. She jumped into her new mum's arms and felt she was the luckiest princess in the whole world.

Shortly after their wedding the king invited his new wife to have a cup of tea in the summer house. As he opened the door, he cried out proudly, 'May I introduce you to the royal parrot!' But before they'd even got past the doorstep the parrot squawked, 'Ugly witch!'

The queen went quite red in the face and started to fidget with her gown.

'Shame on you, how dare you say such a thing!' the king said in dismay.

'Cup of tea, darling?' asked the queen, as if she hadn't heard a thing. 'Sugar, milk?' She made a loud clatter with the spoon as she stirred the tea. 'I say, what a charming room this is,' she rattled on. 'So lovely and sunny and the garden is a picture, don't you think? Will you please pick me some flowers, darling?'

Straightaway the king did as she asked.

As soon as the queen was alone with the parrot she hissed at him, 'How dare you call me a witch! This is outrageous! Just you keep quiet!'

'Most certainly not! Once a witch, always a witch!' screeched the parrot. 'I happen to know who you are!'

The queen promptly choked. Spluttering with rage, she listened as the parrot went on to say, 'You wanted to marry the king! But you were too ugly for that, weren't you?'

'Ugly! How dare you!' screamed the queen.

'Yes, ugly! I know jolly well you've been using magic. I bet you've been eating slushy toadstool soup and drinking cockroach juice.'

The parrot pulled a face. 'And then, of course, you'll have rubbed yourself with snail slime!' the parrot taunted her.

'How did that spell go again?'

She fell for the parrot's trick.

'Mumbo-jumbo-creepy-jeeps,' she answered without thinking. 'Mumbo-jumbo-slikky-slush! Wibble-wobble,crawl right in, wriggle into queenie's skin! Yes, that's the one. That's how I became a beautiful queen! And I'll make sure you don't tell anybody! Ha, I'll cast a spell so you lose your voice!'

She cast a spell but nothing happened.

'Ugly witch!' screeched the parrot.

The queen's eyes blazed with fury. Why didn't it work? 'I'll make you disappear!' she cried. But the parrot just stayed where he was.

'Well, blow me over! What kind of animal is this? I'll turn you into a beetle then!'

'It won't work, so there!' cried the parrot.

He was right. However hard the witch tried, she couldn't turn him into a beetle. Nor an ant, nor a centipede.

And then the king returned, with his arms full of flowers.

At once the parrot called out, 'King, watch out! She's an ugly witch!'

'Now, now, parrot dear, what's come over you?' asked the king, quite upset.

'Darling, I think being shut up in a castle has made him lose his little mind,' said the queen. Wouldn't it be better to let him go?'

The king looked shocked.

'Of course not! He was given to us by a good fairy when Rosalie was born! He's a very special bird...'

Well, I'll be dashed! A present from a fairy! That's why I couldn't put a spell on him, thought the queen angrily. We can't have that!

The next morning the queen crept out to her witch's hut in the woods and made a secret brew.

'Atishoo!' the king sneezed, soon after she arrived home.

'Atishoo!' Rosalie sneezed, and then the footman, 'Atishoo!'

Still sniffing, the king took out his handkerchief.
'What's going on here?'

'Atishoo! I think we've all got parrot allergy,' the queen said quickly.

'But he's been living here these last twenty years!' cried the king. 'And - atishoo! – he's never made me sneeze before!'

The queen sighed. 'Hmm, twenty years, that's just when parrot allergy starts. What a pity, he'll really have to go.'

'No, Dad – atishoo! – he can't go,' Rosalie begged.

But everyone got so sick of all the sneezing that the king just had to think up something. He ordered the footman to shut the parrot in the farthest room in the castle, with two dishes of food and water.

'Ugly witch!' the parrot kept squawking. But no one heard him with all that sneezing. And even if they had, no one would have believed him.

Sneakily the queen quickly cast a spell so that for the time being no one would think of the bird.

Although the king found his new queen very beautiful, it was Rosalie who he loved the best.

Well, dash it, we're not having that, thought the jealous queen.

One day, when she was alone with the princess, she said with feigned surprise,

'I say, isn't your nose crooked, and what a pathetic little mouth you have.'

The princess was horrified. 'Daddy says I'm the most beautiful girl in the world.'

'Dear child, that's what all fathers say. But believe me, you are a most ugly girl. You really are very unlucky, aren't you?'

You could have knocked Rosalie over with a feather.

'Come here and let me comb that hair of yours, it looks such a mess like that.'

The queen sat Rosalie down at the dressing table and looked at her in the mirror. 'Goodness me, I do believe you're cross-eyed... And how did you get that puny little chin?' She twisted Rosalie's hair into two straggly plaits. 'Poor child, it's just too sad. There's nothing to be done. No wonder nobody loves you.'

Rosalie couldn't believe her ears. She was flabbergasted.

'Look at me, dear child,' the queen softly commanded her.

Rosalie looked at her stepmother in the mirror, and the queen's eyes started to shine strangely. The princess felt very sleepy. As if in a dream she heard,

You'll tell no one what I'm about to say

One day, quite soon, you'll go away...

> *Believe me child, no one loves you like before*
> > *Even the king now loves his queen much more.*
> > > *Ugly, ugly Rosalie,*
> > > > *Now you're bewitched, tee-hee-hee!*

The queen snapped her fingers.

In the mirror Rosalie saw a cross-eyed girl with a crooked nose, a puny little chin and straggly hair. She got such a fright that she turned away.
And that's why the princess didn't dare look in the mirror any more.

The next morning the princess's bed was empty. There was just a little note.

'I'm where you can't find me. Because I know I'm ugly and nobody loves me. Bye. Forever. Rosalie.'

The king couldn't believe his eyes.

'*Ugly....nobody loves her...*where's she got that idea from?'
He ordered his army out to search for the princess.
He promised high rewards. But nothing helped.

Rosalie had vanished.

For the second time in his life the king nearly went mad with grief.

'Darling, how terrible for you. Can I help?' The queen stroked his hair and whispered sweet words in his ear.

But inside she burned with glee, because one day the king would forget about his daughter, and she would be First Lady of the land.

If only the king had searched nearer by. Because Rosalie had travelled up dark staircases and shadowy passages in the middle of the night to a room high up in a faraway tower where no one ever came.

And there she was, all alone.

That's why she got such a fright when she saw a little bird on the windowsill. 'Chirp, chirp?'

'Go away,' said the princess sadly.

'Chirp, chirp?'

'GO AWAY!'

The little bird flapped off in alarm to report to his friend the parrot.

'Rosalie, my darling child, where are you?' wailed the king in despair. 'Who can help me?' Suddenly, he had a brainwave - the parrot.

'How stupid of me! Why didn't I think of him before? He always used to help me...!'

The king ran to the faraway room.

'And about time too!' screeched the parrot.

Looking rather ashamed, the king closed the door behind him. He was expecting to sneeze. But nothing came. He looked at the parrot in surprise.

'Silly king, parrot allergy! Ever heard of sneezing powder? That's what that witch sprinkled all over the place!'

'Sneezing powder? That witch? What are you talking about?'

'Listen!' said the parrot. 'And I'll tell you a story...'

'How can you be so sure?' the king asked when the parrot had finished.

'It's just something I knew straightaway.'

'Why didn't you say so before?'

'I did! But you didn't listen!'

The king groaned and covered his face with his hands.

'Oh, how terrible.'

'You can say that again!' the parrot angrily turned away.

There was a long silence.

'Well...' the parrot finally sighed,

'Will you listen to me this time?'

The king ran up the palace stairs, puffing and panting behind the parrot. When they got to the top they pushed open the heavy door of the tower room.

'Rosalie!' the king cried out in a broken voice, and took Rosalie into his arms.

'You don't love me...' she wept.

The king gently wiped away her tears and told her who her stepmother really was. Rosalie didn't believe a thing for, after all, she was still bewitched.

'Come with me,' the king said resolutely.

'What's going on here?' cried the queen, as the door flew open.

'Ugly witch!' snapped the parrot.

The queen said, 'Do be careful, king darling, remember your allergy!'

The king exploded. 'Get out of my sight! I never want to see you again!'

'Nah na na na nah! He never wants to seeheehee you again!' the parrot taunted her.

The queen tried to keep her temper, and said as sweetly as she could, 'But king dear, I love you!'

'You don't love me at all! You're a witch!'

Then the queen dropped her act. Blazing with anger she screamed at the parrot, 'You horrid creature! You sneaky bunch of feathers! It's all your fault!'

She ran, raving and cursing, round the room.

'Now, now, that won't do your looks much good!' squawked the parrot.

This made the queen so terrribly angry that she pulled out her hair and then jumped out of her skin.

Rosalie and the king sprang back in terror. For in the twinkling of an eye the queen had turned into the vicious, hump-backed witch that she had been all along.

'I say, aren't you ugly!' laughed the parrot.

In a burst of fury the witch went for the parrot.

'Guards!' the king called out, pale with fright.

'Forget it! I can magic myself away!'

She flung her arms up in the air defiantly.

But she was so angry her spell didn't work.

'*Stumpy-stompy-dumpy...doop!*'

Nothing happened.

'Hey!' she stamped her foot in irritation. '*Stump-stompy-dumpy...bloop!*'

'Wrong one!' the parrot cackled. The witch stood stock still. She had turned into a statue!

Rosalie looked on, her eyes wide with horror. Her father too was quite speechless.

'Chirp, chirp! cheeped the little bird excitedly. He had a leaf in his beak with a big shiny raindrop on it.

Carefully he laid it on the ground in front of the princess. When Rosalie bent over she saw the reflection of a beautiful girl in the raindrop.

Her face broke into a smile.

With a mischievous look in her eye she went over to the statue, and looked carefully all around it. Then she giggled. 'You're as ugly as you said I was!'

People say the witch statue was placed in the palace garden and still stands there today. Viewing is free – and now you can dare to say anything you like to the ugly old witch!

The End

My name is Sparkle

Make a real princess's crown.

Stick your photo here

Thread a bracelet out of cotton wool balls.

Tie cotton wool onto hairslides to give yourself a special ice hairdo.

Make paper hearts for your hands.

Make your own skirt of ice flowers.

Put on tights.

Ankle band made of cotton wool balls.

Sparkle's ice skirt

What you need:
★ blue body stocking, ballet costume or
long-sleeved sweater ★ pink tights
★ white and/or pink crepe paper
★ about 1 metre of
elastic or ribbon
★ scissors ★ stapler

Put on the body stocking, ballet costume
or sweater. Cut lots of strips of crepe paper.
Staple the strips onto the elastic or ribbon
and tie it around your waist.

Sparkle's ice jewellery

What you need:
★ Cotton wool balls or a strip of cotton wool
★ glue or needle and thread ★ glitter

If you don't have cotton wool balls, then make little balls from the strip of cotton wool.
To make the bracelet and necklace, thread the cotton wool balls together with needle
and thread, or stick them together with glue.
Sprinkle with glitter.

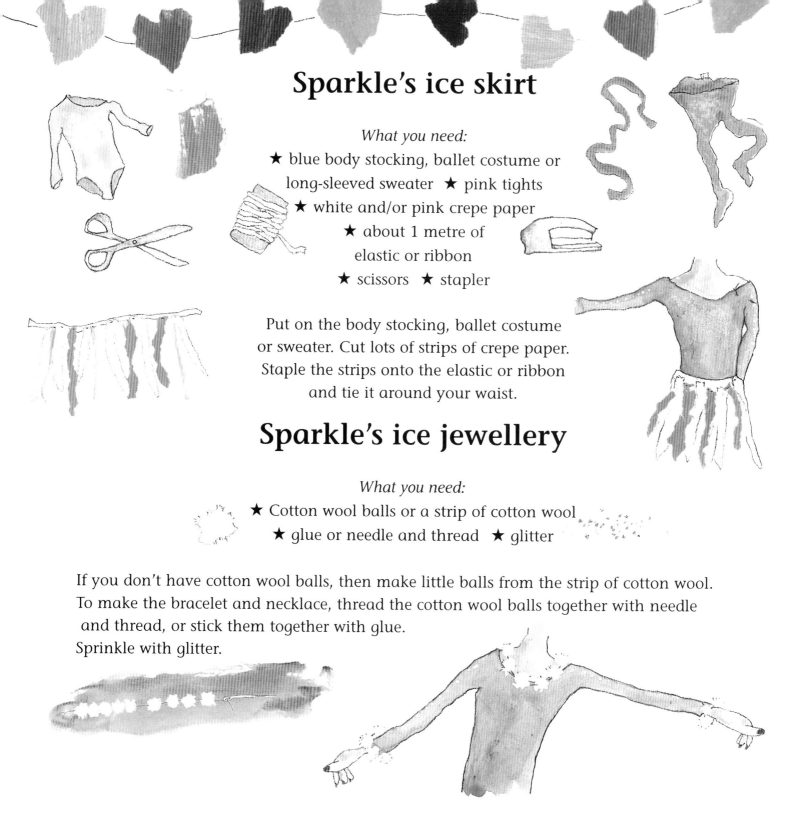

Sparkle's crown

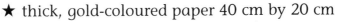

What you need:
★ thick, gold-coloured paper 40 cm by 20 cm
★ Sellotape ★ stapler ★ pencil
★ scissors ★ two strips of material
about 25 cm long
★ cotton wool balls or a strip of
cotton wool to make balls yourself
★ hairslides

Cut the paper into a crown (ask an adult to help you) and join the ends with Sellotape.
Put the crown on your head and mark where your ears touch the sides.

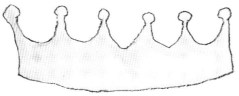

Staple a strip of material where you marked each side.
Put the crown on your head once more and tie the strips of
material together under your chin so the crown won't slip
off your head. You can also tie cotton wool onto
hairslides and fix them in your hair.
This will give you a special ice hairdo.

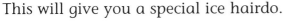
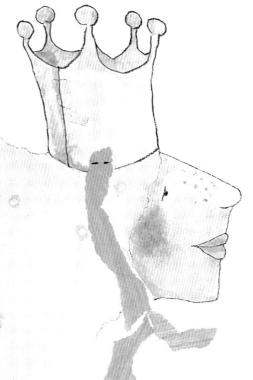

Sparkle's hand decorations

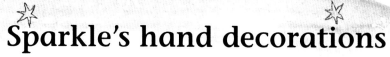

What you need:
★ red sticky paper (or paper coloured red with a felt-tip pen)
★ scissors ★ Sellotape
★ bits of red cardboard

Cut heart shapes out of the red sticky paper. Stick them onto the palm of your hand, close to the base of your fingers.

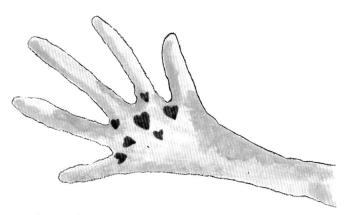

Cut out long fingernails from the red cardboard. Cut a small piece of Sellotape, fold it double and stick the ends together. The Sellotape is now in a ring with the sticky side on the outside. Stick one side onto your fingernail and press the cardboard nail firmly onto it. Repeat this for each nail. As this is a very fiddly job, you might want to ask a grown-up to help you.

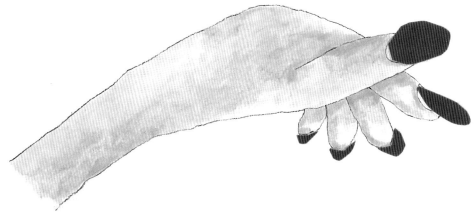

Ice princess customs

Ice princesses like Sparkle love playing amongst the ice floes. You can easily cut these out of white or silver-coloured cardboard. You can make them stand up if you fold them at the bottom.

An ice princess's favourite drink is orange juice or lemonade with lots of ice cubes in it.

Sparkle dances holding ribbons in her hands, because they look so nice whirling around in the air.

Sparkle

Way up north, in a country where ice went on forever
and snow covered the mountains, there once lived a very
special princess. Even if ice flowers covered the windows
and the lake was frozen over, the princess was never cold.
Was that because she was called Sparkle? Or was it because
of her hands? Because they were always as warm as glowing coals.
And if you looked really closely into the palms of her hands you
didn't see just ordinary little lines, but tiny little hearts.

That northern country had no subjects because it was so far away.
  'Why are you king of such a cold and cheerless country?' his wife grumbled
at the king one day. 'I never get to see anybody.'
  'What am I to do about that?' said her husband defiantly. 'I'm not a magician, am I?'
  'May I say something?' asked Sparkle.
  'All right then, out with it,' her father answered irritably.
                    'How about giving a party? Someone's bound to come then.'
                      'What a good idea,' said the king in surprise.
                      'Why did I never think of that myself?'

Dear friend,
I am
having
a party!
Can you
come?

To anybody who wants
to come to a party

Sparkle could hardly wait. With ten days to go, she drew
a star on the wall for each day.

Each evening she crossed one out.

The evening before the party she went to bed extra
early, because morning came quicker that way.

She was so nervous that she couldn't get to sleep.

I know, she thought, I'll count stars, then I'll get
nice and tired.

She pulled open the curtains. 'One, two, three, four...'

In no time at all her eyes were closed. Gently she slipped deep
down into a dream. While she was floating among the stars, all of
a sudden a bewitchingly beautiful lady stood there in front of her.

'Hello, dear princess. I am the Star Fairy. Tomorrow at midnight, when the shower of
a thousand stars rains down, you may make a wish. Now be sure you don't forget.'

She waved her magic wand and vanished out of the dream.

The next morning Sparkle woke up with a smile on her face.

I think I know what I want, she thought.

That day a bitter wind raced across the ice.

All the guests came in with thick coats, double-lined woolly caps, warm gloves and pale faces.

'Brrrrr!' they all cried.

'What does that mean, Mum?' whispered Sparkle.

'They're all cold,' her mother answered.

'Are they really?' Sparkle said in surprise.

Everybody shivered as they huddled up close together, and snuggled deep
down inside their coats. No one said a word.

The king's wife nudged her husband. 'This isn't much fun,'
she whispered. 'Can't you do something...?' The king stood up and
asked, 'Do you know the one about the little polar bear?'

'No,' shivered the guests.

'Listen then,' beamed the king, who just loved any opportunity to make a
speech in front of lots of people. And he told a joke about a little polar bear.

The guests roared with laughter.

'And now we'll have some dancing!' cried the king.

Everyone stood up at once and danced in a long chain behind him – because dancing makes you lovely and warm! The king enjoyed himself no end. Hey, it's great to be king, he thought.

At midnight, when the party was still in full swing, Sparkle cried out in excitement, 'Look, look!'

'Ooh...' a cry of wonder went up from all the guests in the hall.

High above them hundreds of stars were falling from the sky. A sparkling shower of stars came whizzing down without a sound.

'I wish, I wish...' Sparkle whispered fervently. Secretly, everybody did the same. So did the king and queen. When it had stopped raining down stars a great silence descended.

'Ahem,' the king coughed. No one heard him. All eyes were turned dreamily towards the sky. 'Anybody for coffee?' he called out.

'Mmm?' they all sighed absent-mindedly.

'Then off you all go to bed – there's room for you all!' ordered the king. Sleepily everybody shuffled off.

Goodness me, he thought, it's easy to give orders!

The next morning, even before all the guests had left for home, Sparkle ran down the palace staircase and pulled open the heavy door.

'Oh, thank you fairy!' she cried, joyfully. At the bottom of the steps sat a little polar bear, shivering on a silver serving tray.

Sparkle picked him up tenderly. Her hands glowed with warmth.

The little polar bear stopped shivering straightaway and grunted happily instead. 'You'll always be my little friend,' Sparkle whispered.

'And you'll be mine,' grunted the little polar bear.

But, in the meantime, somewhere way up in that northern country, in a wild and wintry ice cave, the Grisly Ice Witch was shrieking,

The Star Fairy, she brings luck,
But stitchywitchie breaks it up!
Stitchywitchie magics heat to ice
one by one, in a thrice!

'Hahahaha!' the witch cackled happily, 'one more!'

'Mummy, mummy!' Sparkle was in tears as she ran into the ice palace. 'We were playing outside and then suddenly little polar bear was gone!'
'Well dear, I expect he was just playing hide-and-seek,' her mother said, trying to comfort her.
'No, no, he vanished – paf – just like that!'
The princess was inconsolable. She searched high and low, but the little bear had vanished into thin air. 'Star Fairy!' begged Sparkle as she lay in bed that night. 'I've got just one more wish, please bring little polar bear back.'
The Star Fairy appeared and said, 'Dear princess, follow your heart and make your own wish come true.'
Sparkle thought furiously. Her hands glowed.
 'If I have to follow my heart, then I'll go out and look for little polar bear right away,' she decided resolutely. Quick as lightning she got dressed and, her heart beating loudly, she rode her reindeer out into the dark night.

A heavy snowstorm was raging across the white ice. Her reindeer could hardly force his way through the snow and wind.
 'Polar bear!' the princess cried out in fear.
 'Cheep-cheep!' she heard suddenly, out of thin air.

The princess looked around in alarm. 'What's that?'

'Cheep-cheep!' she heard once again.

Sparkle couldn't believe her eyes when a frozen-stiff little ostrich popped up out of the snow.

'I say,' Sparkle stammered. 'Aren't you supposed to live on the other side of the world?'

'I'm looking for my friend,' the ostrich shivered. 'The fairy told me to follow my heart, but...it's so c-c-cold here!'

'I've lost my friend too,' Sparkle whispered sorrowfully. As she cradled the little bird in her warm hands, she told him all about the polar bear and the Star Fairy.

Meanwhile, the snowstorm gradually died down. The moon crept out from behind the clouds.

'Oh no it isn't! Oh yes it is!' Sparkle heard suddenly. She looked up. Her mouth dropped open.

A motley gathering of animals were quarrelling in front of a signpost. It said, 'Not to the Ice witch'.

'Are we supposed to follow this signpost or not?' the elephant trumpeted.

'I think so,' snorted the hippo grumpily.

'Should we?' asked the giraffe doubtfully.

'I don't know, I don't know,' squawked the chicken.

The squirrel and the pelican couldn't keep their noses out of it either.

'Whatever are you lot doing here?' Sparkle asked in astonishment, as she made her way over to them.'You don't come from here.'

The hippo was so upset he started to cry.

'We've lost our friends,' he sobbed.

'And the fairy said we had to go and look for them ourselves,' said the elephant tearfully.

Sparkle was amazed. 'Well I never...that's funny...'

'Very funny...' came from somewhere up in the air.

Everybody looked up in surprise.

A snowy owl was circling round above them. 'That witch thinks she's Noah. She collects animals. Two of each kind. But she won't get us!' Everybody watched him, unable to understand.

'Come on, we're nearly there,' said the owl.

He flew round a couple of bends to the left and then a couple of bends to the right. Everybody was nervous as they followed him in procession.

Then they couldn't go any further. A high, jagged-looking ice mountain blocked their way. An ice rabbit stood guard outside a hole in the mountain side. He looked as though he was frozen. He didn't even blink his eyes. The owl just flew right past him into the mountain.

'How scary...' whispered Sparkle. The owl turned round.

'Not at all,' he assured her. 'Because there's something you can do that she can't.' Sparkle didn't understand what he meant. 'What's that then?' she asked curiously. 'You'll find out for yourself,' the owl answered.

Reluctantly Sparkle followed.

The hippo, the elephant and the giraffe looked anxiously at the hole in the mountain side.

'Will we be able to get through?' they wondered out loud.
'Take a deep breath and bend down,' said the owl matter-of-factly.

They just managed to squeeze inside. The smaller animals giggled as they followed them.

A maze of winding tunnels led to the Ice Witch's cave, in the heart of the mountain.

And there she stood, flashing her eyes and stirring a great pot.

'Witchyfixi - animals the whole world wide - Witchyfixi loves you - so just you hop inside.'

'Haven't you got enough?' cried the owl boldly, as he flew into the cave.

The witch looked up angrily. She scowled, her eyes like slits.
'What are you doing here?' she asked crossly.

Sparkle hid in fright behind the elephant's trunk.

Cool as a cucumber the owl flew over to a white curtain and pulled it open with his beak.

A crowd of animals were huddled together, all frozen stiff - behind a row of thick icicle bars.

'How dare you!' the witch screeched furiously at the owl.

Sparkle peeped cautiously round the elephant's trunk.

'Polar bear!' she cried, as she spied her little frozen friend. The witch turned to see where the voice came from.

'Ha! A human child. I haven't got one of those yet!' she cried in delight.

'Ikky-tikky-tees, everybody freeze!'

The elephant, the pelican, the squirrel – all the animals froze statue-still. Except Sparkle and the owl. 'Well, I'll be blowed! Why don't you freeze up?' snapped the witch.

'You don't freeze wise owls at the drop of a hat, that takes time,' spoke the owl from on high.

'We'll just see about that!' Cursing loudly, the Ice Witch threw up her arms.

Horrified, Sparkle crept once more behind the elephant and held tightly onto his trunk.

'Tetteretetteretet!' he trumpeted as he defrosted.

Startled, Sparkle jumped aside. 'What?' she stammered.

'What's she doing?' the witch looked angrily at the owl.

'She can do something you can't do,' the owl answered triumphantly.

'Oh yes? Pooh! *Ikky-tikky-tees, everybody freeze! You're frozen*!' The witch tried once again.

The elephant froze on the spot. But nothing happened to Sparkle.

'Dash, dash and dash again!' The witch charged menacingly at Sparkle.

The princess shrank back. 'No!' she squealed and threw up her arms.

The witch froze in her footsteps.

'Yukkie,' she spluttered in disgust. 'Hearts!'

She stumbled backwards.

'Bravo!' cheered the owl. 'Now do you see what you can do?'

Dazed, Sparkle looked at her hands. They were glowing like coals.

'Oh, is that the secret?' she whispered, as she
saw the hearts sparkling in her hands.
She raised her hands once more and held
them in front of the witch's face.
'Ow, they're hot! I'm not a roasting chicken!'
The witch quickly turned her face away but her nose
was already dripping. 'Dash it!'
She tried to run away but her feet were
disappearing in little puddles of water.
'Go away!' screamed the witch.
But Sparkle bravely stood her ground.

'What a dirty trick!' With a loud screech the witch melted away...
until she was just a bubbling puddle on the ground.

'Now we must....' Sparkle whispered. Hesitantly, she took hold
of the elephant's trunk once again.

'Tetteretetteretet!' he trumpeted right away.

'Yes!' cried the owl, 'and now the rest!'

One by one Sparkle touched the other animals.

'Where is the witch, where is the witch?' squawked the chicken.

'I'll tell you in a minute! Sparkle cried, as she ran to the icicle bars.
The moment she took hold of them, they melted like snow before
the sun. She hurried to the frozen animals. 'Kangaroo, zebra,
cockatoo, monkey...'

Sparkle touched them all in turn. They came to life at once.
In no time at all the whole group of animals were standing
chattering happily together. In their midst was the happiest of
princesses with a little polar bear grunting contentedly in her arms.
When they were all at last outside, the ice rabbit was still
standing guard, stiff as a board.

'Hello rabbit,' said Sparkle in a friendly voice. She stroked his head.
'So,' he mumbled, blinking his eyes, 'no witch?'
'No,' the snowy owl grinned, 'she's just a puddle of water...'

Back at the palace, Sparkle immediately woke
up her parents.
'Mum, Dad!' Stumbling over her
words, she told them what had
happened.
'Well,' her father yawned,
'you have had a marvellous
dream, haven't you?'
'It wasn't a dream, it was real! Look!'
The king and queen opened their eyes.
They jolted upright.
'Hey!' they cried when they saw everybody standing in the doorway.
'This calls for a party!' the king cried enthusiastically.

Hundreds of people came.
The king acted the host beautifully and everyone danced once more in a long chain behind him.
The next day the guests stayed hanging around in front of the palace.
'Actually, we don't want to go. You give such great parties...'
'Stay and live here!' the king cried. 'Then I'll throw a party every week!'

So everybody's wish was granted: for the king a kingdom full of subjects to rule over and for the guests a country full of fun to live in.

The queen was delighted because someone came round every day. Sparkle's new animal friends went back to their own warm countries though, because they suited them better.

'Will you come back for a party now and then?' Sparkle asked.

'Of course we will!' they said, in pleasant surprise.

So, if you're ever way up north and you see ostriches, giraffes or elephants wandering around, then you'll know there's a party on at the Ice Palace!

The End

My name is Oceana

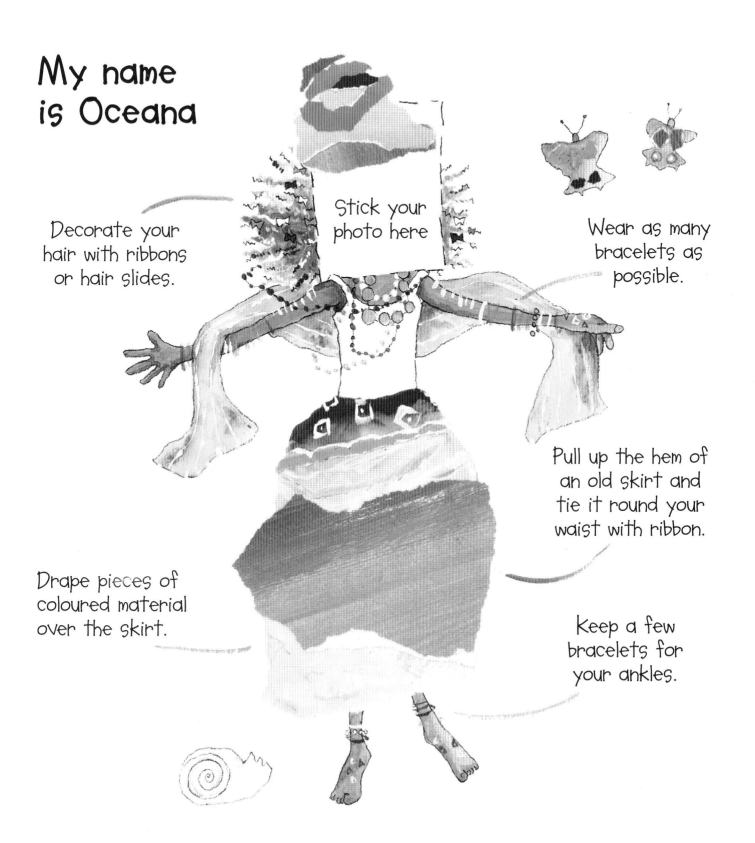

Decorate your hair with ribbons or hair slides.

Stick your photo here

Wear as many bracelets as possible.

Pull up the hem of an old skirt and tie it round your waist with ribbon.

Drape pieces of coloured material over the skirt.

Keep a few bracelets for your ankles.

Oceana's dress

What you need:
★ a ballet costume, white vest or swimsuit ★ ribbon ★ a grown-up's old skirt ★ narrow strips of material about 10 cm wide and 1.5 metres long, such as a couple of old scarves ★ safety pins

What you can also use:
★ beads, buttons, dried beans or uncooked macaroni ★ bits of material or cotton wool ★ 2 potatoes cut in half ★ a knife ★ paint ★ scissors

Put on your ballet costume, vest or swimsuit.
Put the skirt on. Lean down, pull the bottom of the skirt up to your waist and tie it with ribbon (see picture on opposite page).
If you like you can now put the beads, dried beans, buttons and macaroni into the skirt, so that it makes lots of noise when you walk. Or you can put the bits of material or the cotton wool inside, so that your skirt spreads out nice and wide.

Take the scarves or the long strips of material. You can decorate these if you like, but you don't have to. To do this, ask a grown-up to help you cut out a design on half a potato. Dip the potato in paint and print it firmly onto the material. Let the paint dry before you go any further. You can also cut pretty designs out of the material.

Drape the scarves or pieces of material horizontally around your skirt and fasten them on with safety pins. This is a bit tricky, so you may need some help.

Oceana's noisy bracelets and necklaces

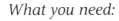
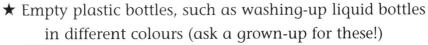
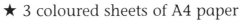

What you need:
★ Empty plastic bottles, such as washing-up liquid bottles in different colours (ask a grown-up for these!)
★ 3 coloured sheets of A4 paper
★ scissors ★ paper clips
★ ribbon ★ glue ★ beads
★ paint and a brush

Together with a grown-up, cut the plastic bottles horizontally into rings to make many bracelets of different widths.
You can also thread the bracelets onto a piece of ribbon to make a necklace (see picture). If you want another kind of necklace, you can hook paper clips together. Stick little bits of coloured paper to the paper clips to make your necklace even more colourful, or thread beads onto the paper clips.
You can thread necklaces and bracelets from coloured beads as well.

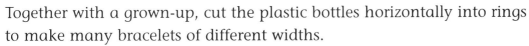
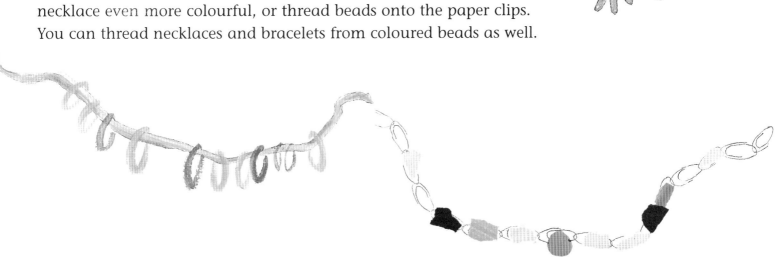

Oceana's hair

What you need:
★ 20 pieces of ribbon
★ 20 hair slides

Tie a ribbon into a little bow on each of 10 hairslides, then fix them into your hair. Without tying them into bows, fix the other ribbons into your hair with more hairslides. Whether you have long or short hair, this will make you look even more like a lovely African princess.

African princess's customs

African princesses like to eat lots of fresh fruit. You can make a delicious fruit salad using lots of different coloured fruits.

African music often has lots of drumming. So make your own music by beating out a rhythm on a drum. Or else bang an old saucepan with a wooden spoon.

Oceana

Once upon a time there was a princess who
lived in a bamboo palace so deep in the jungle
that she had never seen the sea. But she did know a bit about
the sea. Her grandfather told her the most wonderful stories
about it, so in her thoughts she could see the waves and the
magical colours of the water. The princess couldn't understand
why her brothers never listened to the stories.

'Who cares about stories?' said the princes.

'Maybe you can learn something from them,' said
Grandfather. 'Learning makes you clever.'

'Pooh....we're clever already,' the boys bragged. 'We're brilliant at things
like shooting arrows, throwing the javelin, and climbing trees.'

Grandfather looked at them scornfully. 'You do think a lot of yourselves, don't you? But you can't
even see further than the trees, while your little sister knows all about what goes on out there.
You'd better watch out, she's getting so clever, she'll be catching you up before you know it...'

One day there was to be a big party at the palace for the princess's seventh birthday! A very special
occasion indeed in this particular jungle, because on that day she could choose her own name.
The princess had been longing for it to come. She'd known for ages what she wanted to be called...
The name party was to be in the palace garden, but first the princess had a special bath of herbs.

'Mmm, lovely,' she said, as she breathed in the sweet-scented perfume.
'What is it, Mum?'

'Seven-years perfume,' her mother explained.
'It makes you strong.'

After her bath, the princess's skin was painted
with lovely patterns and then she was dressed in
special birthday clothes.

When the princess came out the royal elephants
were ready and waiting. The princess was allowed
to sit on the one in front. She felt very grown-up!

The elephants ambled along, in stately fashion, past a row of
dancing birthday guests all singing at the tops of their voices,
'Mámámámoewè!' to the rhythm of the drum. The princess looked
around her, radiant with joy. Gorgeous decorations were
hanging everywhere.

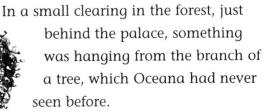

'Oh...' she whispered when she saw a splendidly decorated
birthday chair standing in the garden. 'Is that for me?'

'For you,' said the king. 'A real princess's throne for you
to sit on. But today, as it's your birthday, you are allowed
to stand on it. Up you get.'

'Honoured guests,' spoke the king solemnly, after he had helped
the princess onto her throne, 'today is my daughter's seventh
birthday. She has reached the age when she is to be allowed to
choose her own name! Dear child, tell us what we are to call you from now on?'

Full of expectancy, all eyes were turned towards the princess. She stood up, and said loud and clear,
'Oceana.'

'Beautiful!' the king cried in surprise. He bent down to Oceana and whispered, 'and easy
to remember...'

The princes heard what their father said and were very cross. When they were seven years old, they
had given themselves really smart names. But the problem was that nobody could remember them.
Whoever calls themself Azibjakdoedamoemomowe? Or Bowedjakomoepopotoe? Even the king and
the queen were at a loss, and had to call them just A, B, C and D. The princes were furious! They'd
thought up their smart names all for nothing!

'Oceana, what a silly name,' they muttered jealously. The king raised Oceana's arm on high and
cried importantly, 'Nobody shall ever forget, this child is to be called Oceana!'

'Mámámámoewè!' the guests sang, and then danced over to the baskets full of birthday food.

'Oceana, what a splendid name,' said Grandfather, as he lifted the princess from the throne.

'Come along with me!'

In a small clearing in the forest, just
behind the palace, something
was hanging from the branch of
a tree, which Oceana had never
seen before.

'What's that?' she asked, curiously.

'A princess's swing. My friend the jungle magician made it.
You can feel the waves of the sea in it,' Grandfather explained.
He lifted Oceana onto the swing, and gave her a little push.

'Wheeee...!' the princess giggled as she swung to and fro.

'Hold tight,' said Grandfather, as he pushed a bit harder.

After that Oceana went on her swing every day.
She swung higher and higher.

'Grandad?' she asked one day, 'can you swing
so high you can see over the tree tops?'

'We'll have to ask the magician that,' said Grandfather.
'After all, he made it. And it's time you met him.'

'Oh, how exciting!' Oceana cried. Hand in hand they walked into the jungle. Eventually they
arrived at a simple little house, hidden deep in the forest. In the doorway sat an old man with pure
white hair. A chain of bones and birds' feathers hung round his thin, wrinkled neck. Oceana looked
at him curiously, but his pale eyes looked past her. Suddenly, he said, 'Welcome.'

'I-I thought you couldn't see us,' stammered the princess.

'I may be blind, but I see everything,' said the magician.

'How do you do that?' asked Oceana in surprise.

'I see everything in my thoughts,' the magician answered.

In the middle of the house stood an enormous drum, which was so
beautiful the princess couldn't tear her eyes away from it.

'This drum can answer the magician's questions,' said Grandfather.

Oceana watched how the magician's wrinkled hands played the drum.

'Why do you want to see over the tree tops so much?' he asked her.

'Because I want so much to see what's on the other side,' she sighed
longingly. 'Grandfather told me you can see how the sky touches the earth.
And that there are seas and oceans...'

'How wonderful to meet a little girl from the jungle who is so curious about the world beyond the trees. Lots of people don't even want to look that far,' said the magician. 'But if you know the jungle, then you already know a bit about the sea, did you know that?'

Oceana shook her head.

'Well, you know about tigers and snakes, don't you?' They can be wild and dangerous, but sleepy and lazy too. The sea is just the same: one day it's wild and fierce, the next day it just ripples gently. And just like the iguana, which keeps changing colour, the sea changes colour too: sometimes it's green, sometimes it's blue. Now can you see how the sea is a bit like the jungle?' Oceana frowned.

'Yes, it's difficult, I know,' said the magician. 'And I can well imagine that you'd like to see the real sea. Ask your brothers to push your swing. Because it's through them that you'll reach the world of your dreams...'

Back at the bamboo palace, the princess went at once to ask her brothers if they'd like to push her on her swing.

'Of course,' they said manfully. 'Good for our muscle power.'

But the princess wanted to be pushed the next day too. And the day after that. Higher and higher. She couldn't get enough of it.

'Oh no!' the boys sighed, when they heard Oceana calling again. They decided to push her so hard this time, she'd never pester them again. The princes flexed their muscles and gave the swing one enormous walloping shove.

'Yeeaah!' cried the princess and disappeared amongst the trees. The brothers peered up into the air, their eyes narrowed into tiny slits.

'Oceana! they shouted. 'Ocea-aana...!' Then the swing came back...but no Oceana!

Thoroughly alarmed, the princes climbed right up into the tree tops, but wherever they looked, there was no princess...

They ran back to the palace. Grandfather was alone.

'O-oceana's gone!' Stammering and stuttering, they told their story.

'Hadn't you better go and look for her?' Grandfather answered, without looking up.

'But where? We don't know where she is, do we?' spluttered C.

Grandfather looked at them sternly. 'I thought you were so clever?' Then he relented and said, 'There, there. I know someone who may be able to help.'

'Who's that?' whispered D when the old man appeared in the doorway of his house.

'That is the jungle magician,' said Grandfather. 'He's blind, but he knows everything.'

The brothers looked at the magician suspiciously. A put up his hand. The old man did the same.

'He's not blind,' said the boy. The magician smiled.

'If you put up your hand, then you make the air move. I can feel that. Come on in.'

The boys followed him reluctantly into the dimly-lit house.

As the magician made his way over to the drum, Grandfather said, 'This drum shows him things no one else can see.'

The magician closed his eyes. 'So, boys, has your sister disappeared?'

'Y-yes...' stammered B, in surprise. The magician smiled.

'She's beyond the trees, at the horizon. Wouldn't you like to go and see what it's like there yourselves?'

The boys trembled. They didn't want to go to 'beyond the trees'.

'The jungle's big enough for us.' whispered A.

'Not if you want to find your sister,' said the magician. Gently, he began to play the drum. The comforting sound made the boys sleepy...

An enchanting, velvety light rose from out of the drum. Everything around them went misty...there was just the light and the deep voice of the magician, chanting, *'The sun goes down beyond the trees. So follow the sun, and you shall see...'*

The magician fell silent and stopped playing. The light in the drum went out.

The boys looked in awe at the magician. But his pale eyes looked right past them...

And where was Oceana?

 She had a terrible fright when she fell off her swing and flew through the air, narrowly missing the tree tops. Help, she was falling! But suddenly she felt something slide underneath her. She looked down, and to her amazement she saw that she was sitting on a glossy silken mat which was being carried along by butterflies. Oceana rubbed her eyes...was she dreaming? Carefully she peered over the edge. Beneath her she saw the jungle, like an enormous green blanket, and above her the clear blue sky with here and there a little white cloud. And faraway, in the distance, the sky touched the earth.

 The princess looked around her in delight. How splendid it all was!

 After a while the green blanket came to an end. Instead she saw an endless expanse of blue and green waves moving to and fro. Oceana felt her heart beat furiously. This must be the sea Grandfather was always telling her about!

 The butterflies descended gently and put Oceana down on the warm, white sand. Then they flew away, without a sound. Oceana stood there in bewilderment. She walked towards the surf and stepped into the sparkling water. A moment later a wave gently picked her up.

With their hearts beating in fear, the princes followed the sun. They pushed their way through the dense forest. They badly wanted to find their sister, but this was terrible! They got further and further away from their bamboo palace. There was nothing they recognised any more.

 'I'm scared...' D confessed.

A put an arm round his shoulders. 'We'll b-be all right....'

For some time they had been hearing a strange, roaring noise, which was getting louder and louder. The boys started walking more and more slowly. Now they were in a wood full of palm trees, which had hard, sharp leaves. Meanwhile, the sun had disappeared behind the clouds. A angrily pushed aside a couple of low-hanging palm leaves. 'Stupid leaves!'

'What on earth...?' the brothers cried out. They looked past him and froze with terror as enormous, white monsters foaming at the mouth, came thundering down towards them!

'Shoot them!' C screamed. The boys grabbed their bows and arrows, but to their horror, all the arrows just went straight through the monsters! Just as they were about to run for their lives, B screamed out, 'Oh, look!' They had never seen anything so frightening in their lives. In the middle of the huge, foaming heads sat their little sister!

'Oceana! Hold on! We're coming to save you!' They threw their spears. Just at that moment the monsters let go of the princess and she came sliding, full-length, onto the white sand.

'What are you doing here?' she cried.

'M-monsters!' D squealed with fear, pointing behind her.

Oceana laughed. 'Monsters? Those are waves! That's the sea, nitwit! Ha, ha, monsters!'

The princes started to go red. 'The s-sea?'

'Yes, isn't it fantastic! Just look at the horizon. Can you see the sun slipping from the sky into the sea? Amazing, isn't it?' The boys looked at where Oceana was pointing, where the sun was hanging just above the water like an enormous orange ball. They thought about the magician who had told them about the horizon...and about Grandfather who had said that Oceana would catch them up one of these days...

A looked jealously at his sister, who jumped merrily back into the waves. He took a deep breath and said, 'Come on, we're going to join her.' Followed reluctantly by his brothers, he waded into the sea.

Suddenly, a wave lifted them up on high and their feet were pulled from the sand. They floundered in panic. Another wave came. And then another. They hardly had time to get their breath back as they coughed and spluttered, tumbling up and down in the water. 'You're doing it all wrong!' Oceana cried. 'This is how you do it!' She showed them how to play with the waves so it wasn't scary. Then the princes went tumbling once more into the water, but now they found it much more fun.

Much later, when they arrived back at the bamboo palace, the children ran straight to Grandfather.
'Grandad, Grandad, we've been to the sea!' And they told him the whole story.
'Now you've seen the world beyond the trees, felt the movement of the sea, and seen the sky touch the earth. Isn't it fantastic?' said Grandfather.
B took out a big white shell. 'For you,' he said proudly.
'You've brought me the sea!' Grandfather put the shell against his ear.
The children watched him curiously. He let them each listen in turn. To their amazement, they heard the murmuring of the sea...

The story of Oceana and her brothers spread like wildfire right through the jungle and in no time queues of people were standing in front of the palace – they all wanted to hear the murmuring of the sea with their own ears.
Apparently people are still coming to the palace to listen to the shell. So, if you're ever in the jungle and you see a queue of people waiting, then you may be very close by...

The End